KODIAK

THE PUPPY PLACE

Don't miss any of these other stories by Ellen Miles!

THE PUPPY PLACE

KODIAK

ELLEN
MILES

SCHOLASTIC INC.

For all my malamute friends, past and present

Copyright © 2019 by Ellen Miles
Cover art by Tim O'Brien
Original cover design by Steve Scott

ISBN 978-1-338-57217-9

10 9 8 7 6 5 4 3 2   19 20 21 22 23

Printed in the U.S.A.   40
First printing 2019

CHAPTER ONE

"Wow, I forgot how beautiful it is up here," said Kamila. "Look at the way these huge old trees arch over the road. And the fall colors are amazing."

In the backseat, Lizzie Peterson and her best friend, Maria Santiago, grinned at each other. "Amazing," echoed Lizzie.

They were on their way to the Santiagos' cabin in the country. Lizzie had been there many times before, but always with Maria's parents. This time, they were with Maria's cousin Kamila. She was a grown-up, but just barely—she was twenty-two and had just finished college. Going to the cabin with Kamila felt like a big adventure, and Lizzie was excited.

"When was the last time you were up here?" Maria asked her cousin.

"It has to be, like, eight years ago!" Kamila answered. "I remember I had this new camera I'd gotten for my birthday. I must have taken a thousand pictures. I probably still have some of them. You were the cutest thing, in your little pink overalls. You were such a curious kid, into everything."

Maria laughed. "I remember my pink overalls but I don't remember that trip."

"You sure have grown up a lot since then," said Kamila. "I really appreciate you and Lizzie coming up here with me to help me get settled in."

Kamila was planning to stay at the cabin for a few weeks. She'd asked Maria's parents if she could spend some time there while she decided what she wanted to do next in her life. Maria had told Lizzie that Kamila wasn't sure whether she wanted to be a doctor or a writer. After this weekend, Kamila would drive Lizzie and Maria home, then go back up and be on her own at the cabin in order to figure it all out.

"I still can't believe my parents let me come," said Lizzie. "Maybe my mom just wanted me out of her hair for a while."

"What?" Kamila asked. She met Lizzie's eyes in the rearview mirror. "Why?"

Lizzie shrugged. "She says I've been acting like Eeyore lately, whining and complaining about everything."

"And—have you?" Kamila asked.

"Well, maybe a little," Lizzie said. She didn't know exactly why she'd been feeling so cranky lately, but for some reason it was easier to admit it to Kamila than to her mom.

Kamila laughed. "Hopefully this trip will help you break that habit," she said. "I might even have some ideas that could help."

Kamila turned off the tree-lined highway and onto a narrow, bumpy dirt road. "Almost there!" she said. "We'll have a lot to do when we arrive: unload the car, get firewood, start a fire, get dinner going, set the table . . ."

At home, Lizzie would have groaned if she'd heard a list of chores like that. But the cabin was different. She could hardly wait to get there and get to work. There was something really special about the Santiagos' cozy little cabin in the woods.

The only thing missing on this trip was a dog. Usually Simba would be along. Maria's mom was blind, and she usually had her guide dog, Simba, at her side. He was a total sweetheart, and Lizzie loved it when Mrs. Santiago told her it was okay to pet and cuddle him a bit, when he was off duty.

But since Maria's mom wasn't going to be there this weekend, that meant Simba wasn't, either.

Lizzie would have liked to bring her puppy, Buddy, to the cabin, but that idea had been vetoed by everyone else in the family. The Petersons were all in love with Buddy. Lizzie could just imagine the scene at home: Her two younger brothers, Charles and the Bean, would be squabbling over whose room Buddy would sleep in that night. Mom would be slipping him extra treats "just because," even though Lizzie always told her that he should have to earn them by doing tricks. And Dad would be ruffling Buddy's ears and asking him over and over if he was a good boy. Buddy sure did get plenty of attention at the Petersons' house!

"Buddy face," said Maria, poking Lizzie in the ribs.

"What's that?" asked Kamila, glancing into the rearview mirror.

Lizzie and Maria giggled. "It's just the face Lizzie makes when she's thinking about her puppy—or really about any dog," explained Maria. "Which is basically all the time," she added, with another giggle. Maria knew that Lizzie was totally dog crazy. She'd spent plenty of time in Lizzie's room, which was decorated in everything dog. She knew that Lizzie had dog-themed socks, pajamas, and even underpants, and that Lizzie collected dog books, dog figurines, and of course every color and breed of dog stuffie.

"Lizzie's family fosters puppies," Maria told her cousin. "They've taken care of so many adorable puppies who needed help. They find the best homes for every one of them! Their puppy, Buddy, was a foster puppy at first, but now he's their forever dog."

"That's so cool," said Kamila, smiling at Lizzie

in the mirror. "But isn't it hard to give up the puppies when it's time? I don't think I could handle it."

"It's never easy," admitted Lizzie. "But it helps to know that they're going to great homes. It also helps that we have Buddy."

"Well, those are some lucky pups to have had you in their lives," said Kamila as she turned the car onto an even narrower, bumpier road. "Okay, keep an eye out for the parking spot," she told the girls. "I think it's coming up any minute."

Lizzie loved how you couldn't drive all the way up to the Santiagos' cabin. You had to park at the bottom of a trail and carry everything in. There were two red wagons, stored in a small shed near the parking area, that they used for hauling things. It was a lot of work, but it made visiting the cabin even more special. You really felt like you were in the wilderness. She peered out the window, watching for the big old oak tree that stood by the parking area.

"Wait, slow down!" she said suddenly. "What's that?" She pointed to a flash of white and gray, slipping between the trees on the side of the road. "Whoa! I know there are coyotes around here— but that looks more like a wolf!"

"Where? Where?" asked Maria as Kamila slowed the car down to a crawl. "I don't see it."

Now Lizzie didn't see it, either. Had she been imagining things? She stared into the woods. Yes! There it was again. She spotted a bushy white tail and a pair of pointy ears. "There!" she shouted, pointing. "And you know what? It's not a coyote or a wolf. It's a puppy!"

CHAPTER TWO

Kamila slowed the car down even more as Lizzie stared out the window. Staring back at her from between the trees was a gorgeous young dog. He stood perfectly still just for a moment, so she had a chance to get a good look at him. He had long, thick fur in shades of white, gray, and black; a beautiful fluffy tail that curled up over his back; and a pair of alert, mischievous eyes beneath two furry stand-up ears. Lizzie drew in a breath. That was one handsome dog. He wasn't a tiny puppy, but he wasn't a full-grown dog, either. What was he doing all by himself way out here in the woods?

Kamila pulled the car to a stop. She and Maria both unbuckled their seat belts, and Lizzie saw Maria reach for the door handle. "No, wait!" she cried—but it was too late. The puppy seemed to melt away out of sight, disappearing into the underbrush after one last teasing glance backward over his shoulder.

Ha! You'll never find me. I'm a wild dude, out in the woods.

"Noooo!" said Lizzie, watching him go.

"Where is he?" asked Maria, leaning over Lizzie to look out the window on her side. "I don't see him."

"Neither do I," said Kamila. "Are you sure you saw something?"

Lizzie laughed. "I'm sure," she said. "He's gone

now, but he was right there, by that little cluster of birch trees." She pointed into the woods, which now looked totally empty.

"We can catch him," said Kamila. "If we all get out and walk in that direction, we'll find him in no time."

Lizzie shook her head. "I don't think so. I have a feeling he's pretty shy." She wondered if the dog wore a collar. It was impossible to tell, with that thick ruff of fur around his neck.

"What did he look like?" asked Maria.

Lizzie pictured the beautiful dog. "I'm almost sure he's a malamute," she said. "Like a husky, only different. Their coats and coloring look a lot the same, but malamutes are bigger, with bigger, wider heads. Their ears are set wider apart, and their tails curl up over their backs."

"Right," said Maria. "Okay, so he's a malamute.

And he's also out here all on his own, maybe a stray. How do we catch him, so we can check if he has a collar and tags?"

"Good question," said Lizzie. "I don't want to scare him off, but maybe we should try Kamila's idea. If we fan out a bit in the woods, we might at least catch another glimpse of him."

"Let's try it," said Kamila.

They all got out of the car. Lizzie grabbed her backpack. She knew there was a spare leash in there, and some treats. She liked to always be prepared.

"Let's not get too separated," said Kamila. "We should all keep each other in view as we walk. Your parents would never forgive me if I let you get lost in the wilderness."

They walked into the woods, threading their way through the thick forest. Lizzie looked this way and that, scanning the woods in every direction.

Nothing was moving except high branches that swayed in the breeze above them. All she saw were trees, and all she heard was the loud rustle of dried leaves crunching under her feet. That gave her an idea. She held up her hand. "Stop, everybody. Let's stand still and listen for a moment. Maybe we'll hear him moving."

They froze in place. Lizzie listened as hard as she could, holding her breath. The forest was silent. A big black crow flew overhead, and Lizzie could hear the sound of wind beneath its wings: *whoosh, whoosh, whoosh*. The crow let out one croaky *caw!* and then there was silence again. "Okay, let's walk a little more," Lizzie said. They went on until they came to a fast-moving stream between two steep banks.

"This must be the same stream we cross when we take the path up to the cabin," said Maria. "It's not so easy to cross here, though."

"I think we should head back to the car." Kamila came closer and put an arm across Lizzie's shoulders. "Maybe we'll see the puppy on our way back. Or maybe we'll just have to try to find him tomorrow. But we have a lot of unpacking to do and it's going to get dark soon."

Lizzie nodded, looking down at her feet. She hated to leave that dog outside overnight, if he really was out here alone. "Okay," she said. But she kept an eye out as they walked through the woods back to the car. Once she thought she saw the flash of a white tail, and another time she caught a glimpse of something gray moving, just out of the corner of her eye. But when she looked more closely, she saw only trees and rocks and moss and leaves. Still, she couldn't get rid of the feeling that something was watching *her*. Was the puppy still nearby? Maybe he was curious about these people tromping through the forest.

The drive up to the parking spot took only a few moments. Lizzie helped Maria and Kamila unload their duffel bags, a cooler full of food, and several boxes of Kamila's things. Most of it fit into the two red wagons they had pulled out of the shed. "How about if I stay here with the rest?" Lizzie asked. "I promise I won't budge until you're back, but it's going to take two trips, anyway. Maybe the dog will come to me if I just sit here quietly."

Kamila looked at Lizzie, as if trying to make up her mind. "What would your mom think of that plan?" she asked.

"She'd be okay with it," said Lizzie. "She knows that I keep my promises."

Kamila nodded. "Okay. We'll take this stuff up and unload it quickly, then come right back for you and the rest of the things."

She and Maria each grabbed the handle of one

of the red wagons and headed up the trail, pulling their loads behind them.

Lizzie sat on the big flat rock beneath the oak tree. Its leaves were still green—Mr. Santiago always said that the oak leaves were the last to change. She rummaged around in her backpack and pulled out the leash and the treats. Then, holding a dog biscuit in her open hand, she closed her eyes, slowed her breathing, and waited.

At first she could hear Maria and Kamila talking as they hiked along. Then everything became quiet, so quiet that she could hear the leaves above her rustling in the breeze. Lizzie took a deep breath, enjoying the crisp air. She loved the scent of fall in the country.

Then she heard a different rustling, lower to the ground, very nearby. The sound came closer. Stopped. And started again. Soon the rustling was right beside her.

Lizzie didn't move. She didn't even open her eyes. She just sat as quietly as she could until she felt a wet nose touch her cheek. Then there was a puff of warm breath on the hand that held the biscuit.

"Hi there, cutie," she said as she opened her eyes to see the fluffy puppy sitting next to her. He looked back at her with sparkling eyes as he thumped his fluffy tail on the ground.

How about it, then? Is that treat for me, or what?

CHAPTER THREE

"You caught him!" Maria said when she and Kamila came back down the path.

"Sort of," said Lizzie, ruffling the puppy's furry ears. "Or you could say he caught me." She was already in love with this spirited, happy guy. "Isn't he beautiful?"

Kamila came right over and knelt down to give the puppy a pat. "Oh, he's so soft," she said. "And he looks good, except for these tangles in his fur. He can't have been a stray for long."

"That's what I was thinking," said Lizzie. "And look, he even has a collar on." She parted the thick fur at the puppy's neck to show them the faded red collar he was wearing.

"No tags, though?" asked Maria.

"No tags," said Lizzie. "We can still try to find his owner. Maybe he's been microchipped, but we won't know until we can take him to Dr. Gibson when we get back home." Dr. Gibson was the Petersons' veterinarian. She was always a huge help with their foster puppies.

"Wait a sec," said Kamila. "Don't tell me you're thinking we should bring this puppy up to the cabin with us?"

Lizzie grinned. "Of course I am," she said. "I mean, can we?" Lizzie remembered she was a guest this weekend. "It's up to you since it's not my cabin. But we can't just let him wander around in the woods by himself all night. He may look like a wolf, but he's just a big softie. He'd never survive on his own."

As if to demonstrate, the puppy tried to climb onto Lizzie's lap to give her cheek a snuffle. He was way too big to fit on her lap, but he didn't seem to know that. His legs sprawled out and his tail hung over the side. "Hey," said Lizzie, laughing. "You're kinda big to be a lapdog."

Kamila tilted her head to one side, thinking.

"But before we take him home," Lizzie added, "we'll have to drive down to the store and get him some dog food."

Kamila sighed and shook her head. "First we'll ask at the store if they know about anyone missing a dog. If nobody does, then we can buy some dog food and bring him back with us."

"Deal!" Lizzie said.

"I should have warned you," Maria told her cousin. "If Lizzie finds a puppy who needs help, that's it. She can't stop herself!"

The puppy seemed to know that they were talking about him. He squirmed off Lizzie's lap and went over to sit in front of Kamila. He lifted one big furry paw and put it on her knee, looking up at her with his head tilted.

C'mon, you love me already, don't you?

Kamila smiled down at him. "This guy really is pretty cute," she said finally. "As long as he behaves himself, it shouldn't be a problem."

Lizzie held up one end of the leash she'd had in her backpack. The other end was clipped to the puppy's collar. "I promise to keep a close eye on him," she said.

"Okay, then," said Kamila. "I guess we'd better head to the store."

When Lizzie stood up, the puppy jumped to his

feet as well. He stretched, with his big chunky paws way out in front and his butt in the air. Then he gave himself a long shake.

Great! We're on the move. We've been sitting here FOREVER!

Wagging his white plume of a tail, he charged toward the car, dragging Lizzie along behind him. "I guess he doesn't mind coming with us!" she shouted over her shoulder as she trotted to keep up.

When Lizzie opened the car door, he jumped into the backseat without a second of hesitation. Lizzie and Maria squeezed in on either side of him. His tail draped across Maria's lap, while his big head and one heavy paw lay in Lizzie's. The puppy who had at first seemed so shy was already making himself very much at home.

Maria looked down at him. "I just want to

say, this is not a small puppy," she said.

For some reason, that made all three of them crack up. Lizzie was still giggling as Kamila pulled up in front of the old red house with the GENERAL STORE sign over the door.

"Okay, pup," said Lizzie as she and Maria eased themselves out from under the puppy. She opened her window just a bit to make sure he wouldn't overheat, even though it was cool outside. "You stay for a minute. We'll be right back." He looked at her with begging eyes, but she shook her head. "No dogs in the store." He sighed and lay back down, stretching out full-length along the whole backseat. Lizzie and Maria started to laugh again as they followed Kamila up the stairs to the porch. "That is definitely not a small puppy," repeated Lizzie as she pulled open the door.

The store always looked and smelled exactly the same. Lizzie could never quite remember that smell, but as soon as she walked in it all came back: wood smoke and coffee and cookies baking. It was a cozy place, stuffed full of everything you might need out here in the country, from cans of beans to fishing rods.

"Can I help you find something?" asked the gray-haired woman behind the counter.

"Um, we were wondering," said Kamila, "Has anyone reported a missing malamute?"

"Not that I've heard about," answered the shopkeeper.

"We found a puppy in the woods up by my aunt and uncle's cabin, the Santiagos'. We don't want the puppy to be wandering in the woods all night, so we're taking him back to our cabin. But if you hear of anyone looking for their dog, please let them know we have him."

"Sure, of course. Is there anything else I can help you with?"

"Dog food?" Kamila grinned and shook her head. "I guess we're going to have another guest this weekend," she said.

But Lizzie was already on her way to the far corner of the store. "It's back here," she said.

When Lizzie returned to the counter, lugging a big sack of dog kibble, Kamila grinned at her. "Of course you would know where the dog food is, because of Simba and Buddy," she said.

Lizzie laughed. "Yup," she said. "Also, one time we found three puppies up here! They were abandoned, on the porch of the cabin."

The woman behind the cash register smiled and nodded. "I remember that," she said. She shook her head. "Folks like to drop off their unwanted animals up here in the country. Just last week I found a box full of kittens on the porch one morning. Poor little things."

Lizzie glanced out the store's front window at

the puppy filling up the whole backseat of Kamila's tiny car. She frowned. How could anyone with a heart leave this sweet, giant puppy on the side of a quiet country road, to roam the deep woods on his own?

CHAPTER FOUR

"I hope you like this brand of food," Lizzie said to the fluffy pup as Kamila pulled back into the parking spot at the bottom of the trail to the cabin. They all climbed out, and Lizzie hauled the bag of dog food out of the car and plopped it into one of the red wagons. Then she slung her backpack over her shoulders and took the puppy's leash back from Kamila, who had been holding it.

The puppy had been sitting calmly next to Kamila, watching as Maria and Lizzie loaded up the final items they wanted for the night. Now, as soon as Lizzie was at the other end of the leash again, he zoomed off up the hill, hauling her along. "Hey!" she yelled as the wagon she was pulling with her other hand bounced over roots and rocks. "Take it easy, you wild thing!"

Behind her, she heard Maria and Kamila giggling.

"Ha, ha," said Lizzie. She knew it probably looked kind of funny, especially to her best friend. Maria knew that Lizzie prided herself on her dog-handling and dog-training skills. "Every dog can be trained," she called over her shoulder. "It's just a matter of finding the right way for each dog. Whoops!"

Just before they crossed the rocky streambed, the wagon bounced hard and the bag of dog food tumbled out. Lizzie hauled on the leash with all her strength. "Whoooooaaaaa!" she cried. The puppy barely slowed down, but he looked back at her, his pink tongue lolling out as he gave her a huge, happy grin. "Wooooooo!" He threw his head back as he yodeled, waving his big plume of a tail. Lizzie thought he looked like a howling wolf.

Maria and Kamila laughed even harder, and this time Lizzie joined in. Finally, the puppy slowed down enough for Lizzie to catch her breath. Kamila trotted up and helped Lizzie put the dog food back in the wagon. "Here, I have a free hand," she said. "I'll pull the wagon."

The puppy took off again, and he and Lizzie blasted up the trail in no time, then popped out into the clearing where the Santiagos' cabin stood. The sun had almost set and the sky was growing dark, but there was a glow of yellow light in the cabin's windows, and smoke poured out of its chimney.

"I'm glad Maria and I started a fire in the woodstove and lit some lights on our first trip up, while you were catching the puppy," said Kamila when she joined Lizzie and the puppy in the clearing. "It'll be cozy in there by now."

Lizzie and Maria ran to the cabin door and pushed inside. A cloud of warm, smoky-sweet air seemed to hug Lizzie as she entered. She grinned at Maria and her friend grinned back. They both loved being at the cabin. The puppy looked up at Lizzie and cocked his head, his eyes shining brightly.

Cool place. Okay if I look around?

Lizzie looked down at him. The cabin was so tiny that he really couldn't get into any trouble. Besides the bigger open space, with a kitchen at one end and the woodstove and couches at the other, there were two tiny bedrooms. There wasn't even a bathroom! When she had first come to the cabin, Lizzie wasn't so sure about having to use an outhouse—but she'd gotten used to it.

She let the puppy off his leash and smiled as she watched him dash around, sniffing at everything. Dogs have a special way of getting to know a place.

"This cabin is so great," said Kamila, coming in behind them and shutting the door. She took a deep breath. "I just love the quiet here. No internet, no phone, not even the hum of a refrigerator."

There was no electricity at the cabin. The lights were kerosene lanterns and the fridge ran on gas. Lizzie always forgot how quiet it was. You could hear the wind outside and birds singing in the morning and coyotes howling at night.

"I brought dinner," said Kamila as she hung up her jacket. "I just have to heat it up. Why don't you two get settled in and then set the table?"

"I just need to find Simba's food and water

bowls for the puppy," said Lizzie. "He must be hungry and thirsty after all that running through the woods."

"He can use Simba's bed, too," Maria added. They both knew Simba wouldn't care. He was the most easygoing dog in the world.

Soon, delicious smells began to fill the air, and by the time Kamila said dinner was ready, Lizzie was starving. "This is so delicious," she said as she ate the red beans that Kamila served over rice. The puppy lay at her feet, finally sleepy. "It tastes different from anything I've ever had."

"It's arroz con habichuelas," said Kamila. "My mom's family is from Puerto Rico, and this is the kind of food she grew up with."

"Did you learn how to cook from her?" Lizzie asked.

"Some," said Kamila. "But I learned even more last year when I spent a semester working at a health clinic in the tiny village where my mom's grandparents came from." She passed the pot to Lizzie. "I'm glad you like my food. I brought some ingredients so I can cook more stuff while we're here."

"I remember my dad showed me some of the pictures you posted," said Maria, "from when you were in the village."

Lizzie and Maria kept asking questions, and Kamila told stories about her travels while they ate.

"I would love to go there someday," Maria said.

"What about you, Lizzie?" Kamila asked as they cleaned their plates in the sink afterward. "Where do you dream of traveling?" She pointed to the globe that stood in the corner, next to an overstuffed bookcase.

Lizzie went over to spin the globe. She looked over at the puppy snoozing in the corner. "Alaska," she said, pointing. "Being around a malamute reminds me that I've always wanted to go to Alaska." The puppy jumped up as if he knew she was talking about him. He came over to lean against Lizzie, and she scratched his ears. "The real name of this breed is Alaskan malamute," she told Maria and Kamila. "And they are the state dogs of Alaska." She pictured the malamute on her "Dog Breeds of the World" poster. It showed him at the head of a line of dogs who were pulling a sled over the snow. Lizzie remembered reading that strong, hardy malamutes had been used as sled dogs in the far north since ancient times.

"Cool!" said Kamila. "I hear Alaska is amazing. I have a friend who lives there, way up in the north. There aren't even any roads where she is, at least in winter. You have to get there by boat or airplane or snowmobile—or dogsled!"

"Maybe the puppy should have an Alaskan

name," said Maria. "I mean, if we get to name him."

Lizzie peered closer at the globe. "Anchorage? No. How about Sitka? Or—this is it! Kodiak!" She pointed to a spot on the map, an island in the Gulf of Alaska. "We can call him Kodiak."

"Perfect," said Kamila. She grinned. "There's something special about names that start with *K*, if I do say so myself."

CHAPTER FIVE

That night, Lizzie drifted happily off to sleep with Kodiak at the bottom of her bed. He had curled himself into a tight, furry little ball between Lizzie's feet and the corner where the walls met. *How can such a big puppy make himself so small?* she wondered drowsily as she reached down to pet his soft ears. He was such a sweet boy. Lizzie couldn't wait to see Kodiak and Buddy playing together. She knew they would love each other right away; they both had the same happy, fun-loving personalities. She pictured them wrestling playfully in the backyard. Maybe . . . maybe this would be the time that her parents would agree to adopt another foster puppy, and Kodiak would become not only Buddy's BFF but part of the Peterson family.

The sun was just beginning to rise when she opened her eyes in the morning; shafts of light streamed through the window. When she stretched and yawned, Kodiak woke up, too. He squirmed his way up to give her some snuffly kisses, then rolled onto his back for a belly rub. "Good morning, mister," Lizzie said as she stroked his soft fur.

A second later, he jumped off the bed and gave himself a big shake, ready for the day. Lizzie stretched and yawned one more time, then climbed out of bed herself. Moving quietly so she wouldn't wake Maria, who was still asleep in the other bed, she dressed quickly. "C'mon, Kodiak," she whispered. "Let's go take a little walk."

There was a light on in the main part of the

cabin, and Lizzie saw Kamila sitting on the couch, writing in a notebook. Lizzie didn't say anything; somehow she could tell that Kamila was enjoying her peaceful morning moment. She just smiled and waved, and Kamila smiled and waved back. Lizzie snapped Kodiak's leash on and stepped outside.

It was chilly out, and there was even some frost on the grass. "Brrr," said Lizzie. She smiled at the fluffy pup. "This is your kind of weather, I bet." She knew that his thick coat would keep him warm no matter how cold it got.

They walked around a bit while Kodiak did his business, then Lizzie used the outhouse. When they went back inside, the cabin was warm and cozy. "There's a pot of mint tea on the counter," said Kamila. "Help yourself."

Lizzie made sure Kodiak's water dish was full. She gave him some food, then poured herself a mug of tea.

"Come sit with me," said Kamila, patting the couch. "I wanted to show you something."

Lizzie brought her mug over and settled herself next to Kamila. Kodiak followed her to the couch and curled up on the rug by Kamila's feet.

"This is my gratitude journal," said Kamila, showing Lizzie the book she'd been writing in. "Remember I told you that I had some ideas about how to stop complaining about things? I didn't hear you complaining at all yesterday, but I thought maybe you'd be interested, anyway. This is the way that has worked best for me." She opened the book to show Lizzie a few pages. There were short lists on every page, decorated with colorful swirls and flowers and stars. "Here's yesterday," said Kamila. "Grateful for a beautiful autumn day," she read out loud. "Grateful for this cozy cabin. Grateful for good company." She grinned at Lizzie. "That's you!"

Lizzie smiled. "Cool. But—how does it help?" she asked.

"It just seems like when I pay attention to the good things in my life, the harder things fade away in importance," said Kamila. "My psychology professor in college had us do this as an exercise, because there are a lot of studies showing that practicing gratitude can help your attitude. It really worked for me, and I've been doing it ever since." She reached into a cloth bag by her side and pulled out a small notebook. "I have an extra notebook if you want to try," she said, handing it to Lizzie.

"Really?" Lizzie asked. The notebook was pretty, with gold stars sprinkled over a dark blue cover. "Wow, thanks!" Lizzie opened the book to the first blank page, unsure whether she would be able to think of anything to write, but as she sat quietly next to Kamila the words began to flow. *Grateful for Kodiak*, she wrote, reaching down to give the pup a scratch between the ears. *Grateful for frosty mornings and the cozy cabin. Grateful for Maria. Grateful for Kamila!* Once Lizzie got going, it was almost hard to stop.

Kamila smiled when she saw Lizzie writing. She pointed to an open box of colored markers. "Help yourself," she said. "I love to make every page pretty."

By the time Maria came out of the bedroom, rubbing her eyes, Lizzie had framed her page with flowers and vines. "Morning," Lizzie sang out when she saw her friend.

Maria peered at her. "What are you so happy about?" she asked.

Lizzie looked at Kamila and laughed. "I don't know," she said. "I just feel happy." Maybe this gratitude journal thing really worked!

Kamila jumped up. "I'm going for a quick run,"

she said as she pulled on a pair of running shoes. "Promise me you two won't get into any trouble, okay? I'm responsible for you."

"We won't even leave the yard," Lizzie said, crossing her heart.

After they'd each had a bowl of granola, Lizzie and Maria took Kodiak outside for a walk around the open, grassy area surrounding the cabin.

"See, Kodiak? This is the place where we make fairy houses every time we come here," said Lizzie, showing the puppy the spreading roots of an old maple tree. He snuffled happily, wagging his tail.

I like it here. What else do you want to show me?

"Let's collect some bark and moss," suggested Maria. "If we can't leave the yard, at least we can get started on a fairy house."

The girls walked around the yard, picking up

bits of interesting building materials. "Look at that!" Lizzie said, pointing to a twig on the ground, with a perfect little bird's nest attached. "It must have blown out of a tree." Kodiak, who was sticking right at her heels, gave it a sniff. She let go of his leash for a moment as she carefully picked the nest up in both hands and brought it over to the spot by the maple tree. She laid it down gently. Maria knelt down to look at it.

"It's so beautiful," she said. "Look at the way the sticks are woven together."

"Hey," said Kamila, who had just emerged, panting from the trail. "Where's Kodiak?"

CHAPTER SIX

"What?" Lizzie whirled around. Wasn't Kodiak right behind her?

No. He was not.

He was nowhere in sight.

Kodiak had disappeared.

"Where did he go?" Lizzie asked. She couldn't believe her eyes. How could it have happened? The big fluffy pup had slipped away without a sound.

"He was right there a second ago," said Maria, frowning as she pointed to a spot behind Lizzie. "He was being so good, bringing us sticks in case we needed them for our fairy house."

"But how could he just vanish like that?" asked Kamila.

Lizzie hung her head. "It's my fault. I let go of his leash." She felt terrible, ashamed. What had she been thinking?

Kamila put a hand on her shoulder. "It's okay," she said. "We all make mistakes. The important thing is to learn from them."

Lizzie didn't even want to think about what lessons she might learn from this mistake. She just wanted to find that puppy—now. She cupped her hands around her mouth. "Kodiak!" she shouted. Her heart dropped into her stomach. What was the use of calling? They had only come up with his new name the night before. Plus, the puppy could be anywhere! The cabin was surrounded by woods that went on for a long way in every direction. How were they ever going to find him?

She kicked at the pile of bark she'd so carefully

stacked. Suddenly, it made her feel sick to look at the perfect little bird's nest she'd found.

"Maybe Kodiak is just, you know, a wanderer," Maria said. "Maybe he's always going to want to roam. Even if people have been really, really nice to him."

Lizzie shook her head. She knew malamutes and huskies were famous for loving to run—and run, and run, and run. But she didn't want to think that Kodiak had wanted to leave them. Dogs needed their people, just like people needed dogs, for companionship and comfort and fun. Kodiak already cared for her—and for Maria and Kamila. It was obvious that he felt at home with them. Why would he go away?

"Okay, let's make a plan," said Kamila. She squatted down, picked up a stick, and drew a little map in the dirt. "Here's the house," she said, making a big *X*. "The lake is down that way, and the car is over here, down this trail. You two go toward the parking spot—and stay together! When you get to the car, turn around and come right back up the trail. Don't wander around in the woods. Stay on the trail. Understand?"

Lizzie and Maria nodded.

"I'll go down toward the lake," said Kamila. "I was just running down that way, but who knows? Maybe he cut through the woods. We'll meet back here in fifteen minutes, okay?"

Lizzie and Maria nodded again.

"Don't worry," said Kamila. "We'll find him. Keep calling, and listen for him barking or whining."

"But he's always so quiet," said Maria. "We haven't even heard him bark once."

Kamila shrugged. "Maybe he'll bark if he's in trouble," she said.

Lizzie and Maria headed down the trail. Lizzie scanned the woods as she walked, hoping for a flash of white and gray. "Kodiak!" she called. She thought about how happy and excited she had felt the day before, when they were walking the opposite direction on this same path, toward the cabin. It was so special to be at the cabin with Kamila and Maria, and then to have a foster puppy also! Lizzie pictured Kodiak's furry, perky ears, his beautiful masked face, his happy pink tongue. And oh, that tail! She could just see it, waving like a beautiful plume. "Kodiak!" she called again.

When they got to the stream, they paused for a moment to look up and down its length. "This is where the dog food fell out of the wagon," Lizzie said.

Maria giggled, then put a hand over her mouth. "I'm sorry, but it was funny. Remember how right before that you were yelling at him to 'Whooooaaa!' He hardly slowed down. He just howled back at you. Like this." She threw back her head and *woo-woo-woo*ed like a wolf.

Lizzie wanted to laugh, but she couldn't. Remembering that moment made her miss Kodiak even more. Then she heard something. "Hold on," she said. "Did you hear that?"

Maria cupped an ear to listen. "Um ... hear what?" she asked.

"A howl. In the distance. That way!" Lizzie pointed back toward the cabin. "I heard it. I'm sure!" She threw back her head and howled, even more loudly than Maria had. "WooooOOOOooooaaaah!" she called. Then she held up her hand, listening.

"Wooooo!" came a tiny echo.

Lizzie started to gallop back up the trail. "Come on," she said, waving a hand at Maria. "That's Kodiak. I'm sure of it. Wooooo!" she called over and over as she ran, stumbling over the roots and rocks.

Lizzie and Maria popped out into the clearing

at the same time as Kamila. "I hear howling!" Kamila said. "Was that you guys?"

"It was us—but also Kodiak," said Lizzie, panting. When she caught her breath, she let out another long "WooooOOOOoooooaaah."

"WoooooOOOOooo," came the echo, and this time it was louder.

"See? It sounds like it's coming from behind the cabin," said Lizzie. She dashed around to the back of the cabin, expecting to see the big fluffy puppy grinning at her and waving his tail. But he wasn't there.

Lizzie stood with her back to the cabin and stared into the woods. There was no real trail on this side of the cabin. If Kodiak had run into this part of the forest, they would have to "bushwhack," as Maria's father called it, to find him—push their way through the thick undergrowth. She sighed.

How were they ever going to track down that puppy?

"WoooOOOooo," came a howl—from right behind her!

Lizzie whirled around to look at the cabin. Had Kodiak gotten trapped inside somewhere? "Go inside and check all the rooms," she yelled to Maria and Kamila. "He's right here—somewhere!"

CHAPTER SEVEN

While Maria and Kamila checked inside, Lizzie checked the outhouse. She couldn't imagine how Kodiak might have gotten in there—but you never knew!

The outhouse was empty. That wasn't really a surprise. Lizzie came out and spun around in a circle, wondering where Kodiak was. He was so nearby! "WoooOOOoooaaah," she called softly.

"WooooooOOOoo," came an answering howl.

Lizzie followed the sound, along the back wall of the house. "WooooOOOooaah," she called again.

"WoooOOOOOO!"

"Kodiak!" Lizzie bent down to see the tip of a

nose sticking out from under the cabin. "There you are!" She stood up and cupped her hands around her mouth. "Found him!" she yelled. Then she bent down again. "Are you stuck under there?" she asked. Poor Kodiak! Were they going to have to shovel him out, or figure out a way to lift the cabin?

He shuffled forward a bit, pulling at the dirt with his big paws. But then he stopped. Lizzie saw the whites of his eyes as he glanced to his left. What was scaring the big puppy so much?

"Is it this?" Lizzie asked, touching the handle of a snow shovel that must have been tucked under the cabin for storage. The shovel was light-weight plastic, with a wide yellow blade, and Kodiak easily could have pushed past it. But there must have been something about its shape that frightened him. Lizzie pulled the shovel out of his way. "There you go, sir," she said.

Immediately, Kodiak wriggled out from under the cabin. Kamila and Maria rounded the corner just as he was shaking himself off. His coat was streaked with dirt, but Lizzie, who felt almost dizzy with relief, thought he looked more handsome than ever. He smiled up at them, his big brown eyes dancing. He wagged his plume of a tail.

Hey, thanks! I could've gotten out myself, of course—but it's always nice to have help.

Lizzie, Maria, and Kamila all burst out laughing. "I don't believe it," said Kamila. "He was under there the whole time?"

"Was he stuck?" Maria asked.

"He thought he was," said Lizzie. She told them about the snow shovel she'd moved. "It reminds me of this one time when Buddy thought he couldn't get past the Bean's tricycle. He thought he was trapped in a corner of the garage! Sometimes dogs just get scared of things, for no good reason."

"Well, he's out now," said Kamila, kneeling down to give him a hug. "Let's get this dude cleaned up and bring him inside before he disappears again."

Maria ran for a towel and Simba's brush.

"I wonder why he went under there in the first place," said Kamila.

"Probably chasing something," Lizzie said. "Malamutes have a very high prey drive. That means they want to chase things that are moving. Kind of like this husky we take care of? Misha? He loves to chase squirrels. It's almost impossible to hold him back when he spots one."

Maria was back with the brush and towel. She nodded. "Misha pulled me right over one time," she said, "and dragged me across the yard."

"No more of that while we're here," Kamila said, shaking a finger at Kodiak. "You hear me, young man?" She was smiling. "I'm just so glad he's okay," she said.

After they'd cleaned him up, they took Kodiak inside, where he gulped down a huge drink of water, then collapsed on Simba's bed next to the woodstove.

"I think that experience kind of wore him out," said Lizzie.

"Me, too," said Kamila, plopping down onto the couch. "I think I'm ready for a nap."

Lizzie plopped down next to her. "The funny thing is that if anybody ever wants to teach Kodiak how to skijor or pull a sled, they are going to have to teach him that 'whoooaaah' doesn't mean sing. It means slow down."

"Skijor?" Kamila asked. "What's that?"

Lizzie explained that skijoring was when a person on skis was connected by a long line to a dog in a harness, and the dog helped to pull the person along the snow.

"That sounds like a blast. But does the dog like it?" Kamila asked.

"They love it!" said Lizzie. "Hey," she said, turning to Maria. "That's it! Maybe Kodiak can be a sled dog like Bear, or a skijor dog like Zipper!" Those were two other puppies Lizzie and her family had fostered. Both, like Kodiak, were built for pulling.

"Mm-hmm. Maybe," said Maria. She was at the table, working on a jigsaw puzzle—a big picture of the Eiffel Tower in France.

Lizzie wondered if the people who had adopted each of those puppies would be interested in another dog. As soon as she got home she was going to contact them. Maybe Mom and Dad would even agree to drive up north to see them and let them meet Kodiak! Their family had not taken a road trip together in a long time. "You would love Bear," she said, stroking Kodiak's big broad head. He had climbed up on the couch to squeeze himself between her and Kamila. "Zipper, too. They both love to pull and run, just like you do."

Kodiak looked up at her, tilting his head. He put a big paw on her lap.

Right now I'm very happy to be here with you.

After dinner that night, Lizzie pulled out the notebook Kamila had given her. "Is it okay to write in my gratitude journal more than once a day?" she asked.

"It's a hundred percent okay," said Kamila. "The more gratitude, the better."

Lizzie sat cross-legged on the couch with the book in her lap. She opened it, picked out a gold marker, and wrote, *Grateful that we found Kodiak.*

CHAPTER EIGHT

Kodiak curled up on Lizzie's bed again that night. She liked having him there; it made her not miss Buddy quite so much. But when she woke in the morning, he was gone. She thought about getting up to find him, but she was so cozy underneath her blankets. She could hear rain on the roof, and there was barely any light coming through the window. She knew that Kodiak must be safe, somewhere inside the cabin, since there was no way he could get out on his own. She turned over, pulled her covers up to her chin, and went back to sleep.

When she woke again, it was still raining, and Maria's bed was empty. Maybe it was time to get up. She stumbled out of the bedroom, yawning. The woodstove was clicking away and the cabin was warm.

"Morning, sleepyhead," said Kamila, from the couch.

"Morning! Where's Kodiak?" asked Lizzie.

Kamila pulled aside the blanket next to her. Beneath it was Kodiak, all curled up in a ball of fluffy fur. "We're being cozy together," she said. "I took him out first thing, and gave him breakfast. Then he wanted to go back to sleep."

Lizzie went to pet Kodiak. He was so warm and sleepy that she almost felt like curling up next to him. "What are we going to do all day? It's pouring out there."

"I'm going to finish that puzzle," said Maria.

She was in the kitchen, stirring a pot of oatmeal.

"And there's a ton of board games we can try out," said Kamila, pointing to the pile on a lower shelf. "And if we get really antsy, we can put on our rain jackets, hike down to the car, and take a trip to the store to ask again if anyone's been looking for a dog. By afternoon it will be time to pack up and get you two home."

Lizzie shrugged. "Okay," she said. Every day at the cabin was special, even a rainy day. And on this rainy day, she was sharing the cabin with Maria, Kamila, and Kodiak. What was there to complain about? She reached for her gratitude journal and wrote, *Grateful for a rainy day*. Then she decorated the page with dark purple rain clouds and blue raindrops.

Next to her, Kodiak rolled over on his back and put his paws in the air.

Ahem, all of this relaxing is nice, but I don't suppose anybody around here has time for a belly rub?

Kamila laughed as she petted Kodiak's belly. "I found this spot on his chest that makes him super relaxed and happy when you rub it," she said. "See?" She gave Kodiak's chest a little scratch. His eyes closed and his mouth opened so that his tongue hung out. He gave a long, contented sigh.

"He sure does like you," said Lizzie. She felt a little jealous. Usually she was the one who dogs loved best.

"I like him, too," said Kamila. "I wish my life was more settled, so I could have a dog. Someday it will be."

"Oatmeal's ready," called Maria from the kitchen.

After breakfast, Kamila took Kodiak out for a run. "He doesn't seem to mind the rain, and neither do I," she said as she zipped up her jacket. "As long as we can both come home and curl up by the woodstove."

While she was gone, Lizzie and Maria cleaned up the kitchen, then sat down to try to finish the Eiffel Tower puzzle. "I was thinking," said Maria as she pieced together a white cloud in the middle of the blue sky, "maybe we should let Kodiak stay with Kamila while she's here at the cabin."

"What?" Lizzie stared at her friend. "No way!" She couldn't wait to take Kodiak home and introduce him to Buddy. Kodiak was her foster puppy, not Kamila's. It wasn't like Kamila was going to adopt him or anything.

Maria shrugged. "It was just an idea," she said. "They seem to be getting along so well, and Kamila might be lonely here. Never mind."

They dropped the topic and went on with their puzzle making, but Maria had started Lizzie thinking. Should she agree to the idea? She pictured herself staying alone at the cabin. It was going to be pretty quiet out here in the woods. She had to admit that Kodiak would be very good company.

But—no, he had to come home with her. "How can Kamila take Kodiak before we bring him to Dr. Gibson to make sure he isn't microchipped or tattooed?" Lizzie asked. "We have to make sure Kodiak doesn't have an owner who's looking for him."

Maria shrugged. "That's no problem. Kamila could do that on Monday morning, before she heads back up to the cabin."

Lizzie sighed. Maria had a point. But there were other reasons why she wanted more time with Kodiak. For one, Lizzie knew that her aunt Amanda would have some good ideas about how to train him not to pull so hard on the leash. And Ms.

Dobbins, who ran Caring Paws, the animal shelter where Lizzie volunteered, would probably want to test him on how he interacted with cats. Lizzie knew that some malamutes were not a good match for households with cats. There was so much to do, if Lizzie was going to find the perfect home for Kodiak. Lizzie shook her head. It didn't matter what Maria thought. Kamila was going to have to manage at the cabin on her own—just as she'd planned.

"Whew!" said Kamila as she and Kodiak came through the door, both dripping wet. "It's really pouring right now."

Kodiak walked to the middle of the room and gave himself a huge shake. Water flew in all directions. Some drops even sizzled on the woodstove. Maria and Lizzie laughed, even though he'd done his best to soak them.

Kodiak grinned up at them and shook once more, until his plumy tail was fluffy again and curled up over his back.

We're having such a good time. I love it here!

Maria ran for towels. Kamila dried herself off, smiling the whole time. "Kodiak makes everything fun," she said.

Maria turned to give Lizzie a look. The look said, *See?*

Lizzie saw. She felt something shift inside her, just a little bit. Maybe, just maybe, Maria was right.

CHAPTER NINE

Lizzie watched Kamila and Kodiak carefully for the rest of that day. Would Kamila be able to handle Kodiak all on her own? He was a big, strong dog with a lot of energy. He might be too much for one person. On the other hand, he seemed happy to do whatever Kamila asked him to do. Lizzie had to admit that Kamila had a knack for dog training: She already had Kodiak sitting and shaking hands.

"This pup is a funny guy," Kamila said, petting Kodiak's head as they sprawled next to each other on the couch. "He's got so much drive when he's outdoors, but he's also really good at just being mellow—at least, when he's inside."

Kodiak grinned up at her, thumped his fluffy tail, and opened his mouth wide in a huge yawn.

Exactly right. I know how to take it easy.

"Finished!" said Maria, just then. She stuck one last puzzle piece into place and sat back, both thumbs up. "Yay, me!"

"Yay, you!" said Kamila, getting up to take a look. "Hey, that's beautiful. Nice job."

Kodiak had followed Kamila. He put his paws up on Maria's lap as if he wanted to look at the puzzle, too.

Can I see?

Maria laughed. "I'm sure it's not a good idea to let you do this, but I get it. You want to check out the Eiffel Tower, right?" She put her arm around Kodiak as he looked at the puzzle. She leaned her cheek against his and sighed. "I wish all four of us could just stay at the cabin for, like, a month. It's so peaceful here."

"Wouldn't you get bored?" asked Kamila.

Maria shook her head. "No way. There's so much to do here," she said. "Fairy houses and puzzles and games and hikes and swimming in the summer . . ."

"Plus, if Kodiak was with us, he would keep us busy," said Lizzie.

"Sounds good to me," said Kamila. "But, um, isn't there this thing called school? You know, like, a place where you're supposed to go every day? And weren't you telling me about your dog-walking business? What about all your clients? You wouldn't just leave them for a month."

"You're right," Lizzie said. "But we don't have to

go back quite yet, right? Let's play Monopoly. And maybe make some brownies—I saw a mix in the cupboard."

Lizzie knew she would always remember the rest of that cozy afternoon at the cabin. She and Maria and Kamila played games. They drank cocoa and ate brownies, and they took Kodiak for walks in the rain. They wrote in their gratitude journals—Maria had started one, too—and they cuddled with Kodiak, and they leafed through old magazines, laughing at the weird fashions from the '80s. Finally, they packed up their things into the red wagons (thankfully, the rain had stopped by then), and went down the trail to the car. On their way home they stopped at the store to check if anyone had reported a lost dog—they hadn't—and to leave a sign about Kodiak, including their contact information.

"That was the best time I've ever had at the

cabin," Lizzie said as Kamila pulled up in front of the Petersons' house later that afternoon. She took hold of Kodiak's leash and got ready to climb out of the car. Then she froze. "Oh, no!" she said, putting a hand over mouth. "I just realized something. I never had a chance to tell Mom and Dad that I was bringing home a foster puppy!"

Kamila laughed. "It's okay," she said. "I shot off a quick e-mail when we were at the store. They should be prepared. But just in case, maybe I'll walk you in and say hello."

The front door opened just then. Mom waved and smiled. "Welcome home! Buddy's in the backyard," she said. "He's eager to meet his new foster brother."

They all went around back. The moment they were inside the fenced yard, Buddy came charging over, wagging his tail. He was always so friendly to their foster animals.

Kodiak stood stiffly, very close to Kamila's leg. He let Buddy sniff him, but he stood still as a statue, except for some tiny tail wags.

"I think he hasn't been around another dog for a while," said Lizzie. "Give him some time, Buddy. He's a little shy."

Buddy backed off and sat down, but only for a second. He jumped up and went into a play bow, front legs outstretched.

Kodiak glanced up at Kamila.

What do you think? Is it safe?

"Go ahead," she said, unclipping his leash. "Go play."

A second later the two pups were racing around the yard, stopping only to wrestle and tumble in the grass.

"I knew they'd get along," said Lizzie. She loved

to watch Buddy playing with other dogs. It made him so happy to chase and be chased, to jump and tussle.

Mom came outside to give Lizzie a hug. "Did you have fun?" she asked.

"It was the best," said Lizzie, smiling up at her. She was happy to see Mom.

"Wow, Kodiak is adorable. And look how much he and Buddy like each other already," said Mom. She and Lizzie watched the puppies play.

"Lizzie and Maria were a huge help," Kamila told Mom. "They jumped right in on the cooking and cleaning without me even having to ask."

Mom turned to look at Lizzie, eyebrows raised. "Really?" she asked. "That's good to hear."

Lizzie knew what the quizzical look on Mom's face meant. It meant, *Why can't you be that way at home?*

"It's fun at the cabin," Lizzie said, shrugging.

"I should get going," said Kamila. Kodiak had run over to her side, as if to say goodbye. She bent over to give him a huge hug, then straightened up. Lizzie saw tears sparkling in her eyes.

Mom put her arm around Kamila's shoulders. "Thanks for taking care of my girl," she said. "And thanks for delivering our new foster pup."

"Um, Mom?" Lizzie said. She paused and bit her lip. She looked over at Maria, and Maria nodded encouragingly. Lizzie nodded back. It was hard, but she knew it was the right thing. "You got that last thing wrong. Kodiak isn't our foster dog. He's Kamila's."

CHAPTER TEN

At dinner that night, Lizzie sat and stared at her plate. She poked at a meatball and toyed with some spaghetti.

"Lizzie, are you going to eat your dinner or play with it?" asked Dad.

"I'm not hungry," she said.

"Too much junk food from the store?" Mom asked, passing the salad to Dad. She knew what Lizzie and Maria usually ate when they were up at the cabin.

"We didn't have any!" Lizzie said. "Kamila is a really good cook."

"So is your mother," said Dad.

Charles nodded. "It's really good, Mom," he said.

The Bean waved a forkful of spaghetti. "Yum!" he said. His whole face was red with sauce.

"If you're not going to eat, maybe you can wipe your brother's face," said Mom, passing Lizzie a napkin.

"I always have to do all the cleaning up," Lizzie grumbled. She took the napkin and dabbed at the Bean's face. He grinned at her and she couldn't help smiling back. The Bean was pretty cute.

But he wasn't a puppy. He wasn't a big, happy, furry malamute.

"There will be other foster puppies," Mom said gently.

Lizzie didn't always like it when her mom read her mind. "But not another Kodiak," she said, crossing her arms. "You don't even know what a great dog he is."

"And he'll be great company for Kamila," said

Dad. "You were very generous to let her take him. I know she'll really appreciate having him with her at the cabin."

"I know, I know, I know, I know, I know," said Lizzie. She pushed back her chair. "May I be excused?"

"If you're going to be such a grumpy-pants, maybe it's just as well for you to spend some time in your room," said Mom, nodding. "Go ahead."

Lizzie took her plate to the kitchen and left it on the counter. Then she grabbed the backpack she'd taken to the cabin and stomped upstairs. She shut the door to her room and emptied the whole backpack on the bed, looking for her pajamas. A gleam of gold caught her eye and she fished out her gratitude journal. Ha. What did she have to be grateful for? No Kodiak. No more of Kamila's delicious family recipes, or cozy cabin or fun board games. Miserable, Lizzie flopped down on top of all the stuff she'd unpacked.

A few moments later, Mom knocked softly on the door. "Lizzie?" she asked as she sat down next to Lizzie on the bed. "Sweetie, what's the matter? I hate to see you this way."

"I've just been feeling sad, Mom. I don't know why," Lizzie said.

"Sometimes that happens. But I'm always here for you to talk to. I'm always here to listen," Mom said.

Lizzie had thrown the blanket over her head. She wouldn't look at Mom.

"Your dad and I love you very much. And when you need to talk to us, we'll be here for you. We're always here for you. The whole family is." Mom put her hand on Lizzie's back and rubbed gently.

Lizzie came out from under the blanket. "Really?" she asked.

Later that night, before she turned out her lights, Lizzie reached for her gratitude journal. *Grateful to have a mom who listens to me*, she wrote. *Grateful that Kodiak and Kamila are together.*

Lizzie wrote in her gratitude journal every night that week.

Monday: Grateful for Buddy. I still love him best, anyway.

Tuesday: Grateful for getting 100% on my math quiz. Grateful for Buddy.

Wednesday: Grateful for a sunny day. Grateful for Buddy. Grateful that Kamila promised to bring Kodiak for a visit on Saturday.

Thursday: Grateful for Buddy. Grateful that Saturday is only two days away.

On Friday night after dinner, Lizzie and her family were playing twenty questions. Lizzie liked that game because you didn't need a board or dice or cards or anything. All you did was think of something, and then the other people tried to guess what it was, in twenty questions. Whoever guessed got to be the next person who thought of the thing.

"Animal, vegetable, or mineral?" Lizzie asked Charles. That was always the first question. Animals could be dogs, cats, lizards, and even—most often—people. That was weird, but it was the way the game worked. Vegetables could be things like a tree, a wooden toy, or a flower in the garden. And minerals were things like phones or cars, items that were made out of materials that came from the earth, like iron, or were totally created by people in laboratories.

"Um," said Charles, pretending to think about

her question. He was always trying to bluff, to act like something was a hard question when it wasn't. "Animal," he said, after a moment.

Lizzie nodded. That meant it was probably either Buddy or some other dog, or it was a person—a famous baseball player, or maybe just Dad. She wanted to ask another question right away, but it was Mom's turn.

"Are you Buddy?" Mom asked.

Lizzie gave Mom a secret little smile that said, *We know Charles, don't we?*

"Nope," said Charles, shaking his head.

"Are you on the Red Sox?" Dad asked.

Charles laughed. "Uh-uh," he said. "That's a definite no."

Lizzie jumped a little in her seat. She knew who it was. Sammy, Charles's best friend who lived next door. But it was the Bean's turn.

"Are you a tarrot?" the Bean asked.

"A parrot?!" Charles asked.

The Bean shook his head. "A tarrot. Like you eat." He made a motion like Bugs Bunny, eating a carrot.

Giggling, Charles said he was not. "A carrot is not an animal, anyway," he told the Bean. "It's a vegetable."

"Are you—" Lizzie began, but then the doorbell rang.

"I'll get it!" said Charles, leaping up.

Lizzie could tell that her brother was trying to get away before she could get her next question out. Now she knew for sure that she was right about Charles's "animal" being Sammy. Plus, Lizzie knew that Charles knew that she knew.

Lizzie heard the door open. Then she heard the scrabble of paws on the front hall floor. A moment later, Kodiak galloped into the room, tossing his big head and wagging his beautiful feathery tail.

"Kodiak!" Lizzie threw her arms around him, and Kodiak snuffled her cheek. Buddy jumped up from his bed to greet his friend, and the dogs sniffed each other with wagging tails.

"He couldn't wait to see you." Kamila came into the room, smiling. "He remembered that this was your house and started *woo-woo*ing when we pulled up."

"But—what are you doing here?" Lizzie asked. "You weren't supposed to come till tomorrow. Was he too much for you?"

Kamila grinned. "No, he was just perfect for me. He helped me make a big decision in a hurry. Kodiak and I are going to Alaska together!" She paused. "I mean, if that's okay with you, Lizzie. I'd like to adopt this wild and cuddly dude."

Lizzie stared at Kamila. "Alaska?"

"I found a job where my friend lives, helping out at a clinic. And I'm going to blog about my experiences in Alaska—I might even do it from Kodiak's point of view, just for fun. Anyway, I'm going to see what it's like to be a doctor *and* a writer. Maybe I can do both." She ruffled Kodiak's ears. "Plus, I definitely want to try sledding or skijoring with this guy."

"But how are you getting there?" Lizzie asked.

"That's the best part," said Kamila. "C'mere, I'll show you." She jumped up and Lizzie followed her to the front door. Kodiak and Buddy ran with them. Kamila opened the door and waved a hand. "Ta-da!" she said. "I traded my car for that. Kodiak and I are going on a road trip together!" Parked in front of the house was a white van, painted with sunflowers. It had yellow curtains at the back windows. "I mean, like I said, if you say it's okay for me to adopt Kodiak." Kamila gave Lizzie a serious look.

Lizzie felt a pang. Kodiak and Kamila were

headed off on an amazing adventure—that is, they were if she said yes to Kamila adopting Kodiak. It only took her a moment to speak up. "That's so cool," she said. "I'm jealous. You're going to have so much fun. Of course you should adopt Kodiak. You two are great together."

"Really?" Kamila swept Lizzie into a big hug. "I'll always be grateful for you," she said into Lizzie's ear. "Maybe you'll come visit us in Alaska someday."

"Maybe?" Lizzie asked. "Definitely." She could just picture Kodiak and Kamila dashing through the snow together, with pine trees and beautiful mountains in the background. The two of them were meant to be best friends forever.

Lizzie hugged Kamila back. "I'm grateful for *you*," she said.

PUPPY TIPS

It can be very difficult to train a dog not to pull on the leash, especially one that is bred for pulling, like a malamute. I know, because I've tried so many times to teach my dog, Zipper, to walk nicely on a leash. Some dogs learn easily, and there are many techniques to try (you can find them in dog-training books or online) using positive reinforcement—that is, rewards for good behavior, not punishment for "bad" behavior. In the end, the things that have worked best for Zipper are head collars and no-pull harnesses, which keep him from pulling without me having to jerk on his neck or make him wear a prong collar. If you have a dog who pulls, you might want to try one of these, too. There are a few different brands and you can research them online or ask your vet or a dog trainer for a recommendation.

Dear Reader,

The part in this story where Kodiak disappears comes straight from something that happened with my dog, Zipper. One day he disappeared from the yard, and I couldn't find him anywhere. I called and whistled and walked all the paths that we usually walk, but there was no sign of him. I was really worried, and I sat down on the front porch to figure out what to do next. Then I heard a tiny little whimper that told me he was nearby, maybe somewhere in back of the house. I was looking and looking and still couldn't find him until he whined again—and there he was, under the back porch! Just like Kodiak, he thought he was stuck because there was a snow shovel that was sort of in his way, and as soon as I pulled it out he squirmed out from under the porch. He was so happy—and I was, too!

Yours from the Puppy Place,
Ellen Miles

ABOUT THE AUTHOR

Ellen Miles loves dogs, which is why she has a great time writing the Puppy Place books. And guess what? She loves cats, too! (In fact, her very first pet was a beautiful tortoiseshell cat named Jenny.) That's why she came up with the Kitty Corner series. Ellen lives in Vermont and loves to be outdoors with her dog, Zipper, every day, walking, biking, skiing, or swimming, depending on the season. She also loves to read, cook, explore her beautiful state, play with dogs, and hang out with friends and family.

Visit Ellen at ellenmiles.net.

THE PUPPY PLACE

READ THEM ALL!

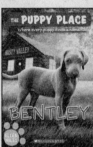

- ❏ Angel
- ❏ Bandit
- ❏ Barney
- ❏ Baxter
- ❏ Bear
- ❏ Bella
- ❏ Bentley
- ❏ Bitsy
- ❏ Bonita
- ❏ Boomer
- ❏ Bubbles and Boo
- ❏ Buddy
- ❏ Champ
- ❏ Chewy and Chica

- ❏ Cocoa
- ❏ Cody
- ❏ Cooper
- ❏ Daisy
- ❏ Edward
- ❏ Flash
- ❏ Gizmo
- ❏ Goldie
- ❏ Gus
- ❏ Honey
- ❏ Jack
- ❏ Jake
- ❏ Kodiak
- ❏ Liberty
- ❏ Lola
- ❏ Louie

- ❏ Lucky
- ❏ Lucy
- ❏ Maggie and Max
- ❏ Mocha
- ❏ Molly
- ❏ Moose
- ❏ Muttley
- ❏ Nala
- ❏ Noodle
- ❏ Oscar
- ❏ Patches
- ❏ Princess
- ❏ Pugsley
- ❏ Rascal
- ❏ Rocky

- ❏ Roxy
- ❏ Rusty
- ❏ Scout
- ❏ Shadow
- ❏ Snowball
- ❏ Spirit
- ❏ Stella
- ❏ Sugar, Gummi, and Lollipop
- ❏ Sweetie
- ❏ Teddy
- ❏ Winnie
- ❏ Ziggy
- ❏ Zipper

■ SCHOLASTIC

scholastic.com